**DATE DUE**

| | | |
|---|---|---|
| S. BARAD 4-5 '79 | | |
| S. BAR A 4 - 5 '79 | | |
| FT. JO B 9/6 - '79 | | |
| MONTA A 4 8 '81 | | |
| GREN A 10 20 '81 | | |
| KLA. R A 1 0 22 81 | | |
| T. JO J 8 31 '83 | | |
| A 2 28 '84 | | |
| IL. C A 9 - 3 '86 | | |
| 17 '87 | | |

PRINTED IN U.S.A.

D0688944

PROPERTY OF
SISKIYOU COUNTY
SCHOOLS LIBRARY

398.2
Duf
c.1         Duff, Maggie                    35389

            Rum Pum Pum

Siskiyou County Schools Library
Yreka, California

# Rum Pum Pum

A folk tale from India                retold by Maggie Duff

## Pictures by Jose Aruego and Ariane Dewey

35389

MACMILLAN PUBLISHING CO., INC.

New York

COLLIER MACMILLAN PUBLISHERS

London

Siskiyou County
Schools Library

*To John Mitchell, my first devoted listener; to the children of Gates Mills who have listened with such pleasure to my tellings of tales; and last but not least, to my husband, who evoked my interest in kettledrums.*  — M.D.

*To Juan*
— A.D. and J.A.

Copyright © 1978 Maggie Duff / Copyright © 1978 Jose Aruego and Ariane Dewey
All rights reserved. No part of this book may be reproduced or transmitted in any form or by any means, electronic or mechanical, including photocopying, recording or by any information storage and retrieval system, without permission in writing from the Publisher.

Macmillan Publishing Co., Inc., 866 Third Avenue, New York, N.Y. 10022 / Collier Macmillan Canada, Ltd.
Printed in the United States of America

10 9 8 7 6 5 4 3 2 1

LIBRARY OF CONGRESS CATALOGING IN PUBLICATION DATA
Duff, Maggie. Rum pum pum.
SUMMARY: Aided by others who have suffered at the hands of the King, a blackbird seeks revenge on the monarch who has stolen his wife.
[1. Folklore — India] I. Aruego, Jose. II. Dewey, Ariane. III. Title.
PZ8.1.D84Ru 1978 [398.2] [E] 77-12389 ISBN 0-02-732950-X

Long ago in India a blackbird lived with his mate in a tree.
Blackbird sang very sweetly.

One day the King heard him as he was passing by.

"Bring me that sweet-singing blackbird," said the King. "I will keep him in a cage in my palace."

So the King's men set out to capture Blackbird; but they caught his wife by mistake, for they looked exactly alike and the King's men couldn't tell the difference.

When Blackbird discovered his wife had been stolen, he was very angry.
He decided to get her back by whatever means.

Blackbird tied a long, sharp thorn
around his waist for a sword.

He took the skin of a dead frog
to use as a shield.

On his head he put half a walnut
shell for a helmet,

and made the other half into a kettledrum
by stretching a piece of skin across it.

Then he declared war on the King. Down the road he marched, beating his drum, RUM PUM PUM, RUM PUM PUM, RUM PUM PUM PUM PUM.

Before long he met a cat.

"Where to?" asked Cat.

"To make war on the King. He stole my wife."

"I'll join you. The King drowned my kittens."

"Jump into my ear then," said Blackbird.

So Cat jumped into Blackbird's ear, curled up and went to sleep.

Rum Pum Pum

Blackbird marched on, beating his drum as he went,
RUM PUM PUM, RUM PUM PUM, RUM PUM PUM
PUM PUM. Soon he met some ants.

"Where to?" asked the ants.

"To make war on the King. He stole my wife."

"We'll join you. The King poured boiling water into our hill."

"Crawl into my ear then," said Blackbird. The ants did.

Blackbird marched on down the road beating his drum, RUM PUM PUM, RUM PUM PUM, RUM PUM PUM PUM PUM, until he met a stick.

"Where to?" asked Stick.

"To make war on the King. He stole my wife."

"I'll join you. The King tore me from my tree in a fit of temper."

"Get into my ear then," said Blackbird. So Stick did.

Siskiyou County
Schools Library

Not far from the King's palace Blackbird had to cross
a river.

"Where to?" asked River.

"To make war on the King. He stole my wife."

"Then I will join you. The King has let my waters
become polluted."

"Flow into my ear," said Blackbird.

As you can well imagine, Blackbird's ear was really
full by now, but somehow River found a place.

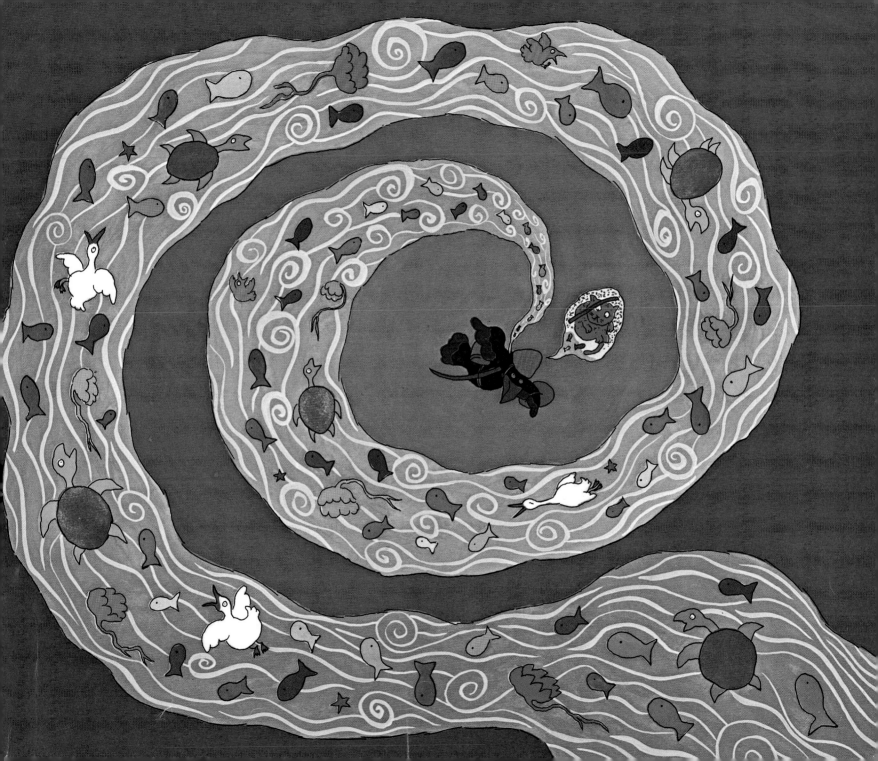

Then, RUM PUM PUM, RUM PUM PUM, RUM PUM
PUM PUM PUM, Blackbird marched right up to the palace gates.
THUMP THUMP THUMP, he knocked at the door.

"Who's there?" called out the gatekeeper.

"General Blackbird here," answered Blackbird, "come to
make war on the King and get back his wife."

The gatekeeper looked out. When he saw Blackbird standing
there with his thorn sword, frog-skin shield, helmet made
from half a walnut shell, and carrying a kettledrum made
from the other half, he laughed so hard he nearly fell off his
stool. He had never in all his life seen anything so funny!

But after that he opened the gate and took Blackbird into
the King's presence.

Rum Pum Pum...

"What do you want?" demanded the King.

"I want my wife," said Blackbird.

"Well, you shan't have her," the King answered crossly.

"Then you will have to take the consequences," said Blackbird.

And with that he marched around the room beating his kettledrum, RUM PUM PUM, RUM PUM PUM, RUM PUM PUM PUM PUM.

"Seize that insolent fellow and throw him into the henhouse tonight!" shouted the King. "Those hens will make short work of him."

So the King's men seized Blackbird.

That night when they threw him into the henhouse, the hens were already asleep. When all was quiet and everyone asleep in the palace, Blackbird sang out softly,

"Come out, Catkin, come out of my ear,
There are hens a-plenty here.
Chase them till their feathers fly,
Claw them as they flutter by."

So out came Cat to chase the hens. Such a squawking and running about! When they had all fluttered through the door and were out of sight, Cat jumped back into Blackbird's ear and went to sleep.

Next morning the King sent for a report. When he heard that the hens were all gone and Blackbird was marching around the henhouse beating on his drum, RUM PUM PUM, RUM PUM PUM, RUM PUM PUM PUM PUM, he was very angry indeed.

"Take that impudent bird tonight and throw him into the stables where the wild horses are," shouted the King. "They'll soon finish him off."

So that night the King's men threw Blackbird in with the wild horses, but he flew up to the rafters before they could touch him. When all was quiet and everyone asleep in the palace, Blackbird sang out softly,

> "Come out of my ear and help me, Stick.
> Beat the horses to make them kick.
> Beat them till at dawn of day
> They break the door and run away."

Out came Stick and did just that. Then back into Blackbird's ear Stick went.

When it was morning, the King sent for Blackbird's
remains. Instead of remains, the King's men found the
horses gone and Blackbird marching around the stables beating
his drum, RUM PUM PUM, RUM PUM PUM, RUM
PUM PUM PUM PUM.

The King was furious. The horses had cost a lot of money.

"Throw that fellow into the elephants' pen tonight," shouted
the King. "That will be the end of him."

So that night Blackbird was put into the elephants' pen.
But before the sleepy elephants could waken to trample him,
Blackbird found a safe place to hide. When all was quiet and
everyone asleep in the palace, Blackbird sang out softly,

"Come out of my ear and help me, ants.
Crawl up the trunks of the elephants.
Sting them, bite them on the head,
Bite them till they fall down dead."

Out crawled the ants, right up the trunks of the elephants.
They stung and bit the elephants on the head until they went
quite mad and trampled each other. When they all lay dead,
the ants crawled back into Blackbird's ear.

Siskiyou County
Schools Library

In the morning the King himself went to collect Blackbird's carcass. When he found the elephants all dead and Blackbird marching around beating his kettledrum, RUM PUM PUM, RUM PUM PUM, RUM PUM PUM PUM PUM PUM, the King was not only furious, he was desperate!

"I don't know how that fellow does it," he said, "but I must find out. Tonight tie him to my bedpost, and then we will see what we will see."

So that night Blackbird was tied to the King's bedpost. When all was quiet and everyone asleep in the palace (except the King, who only pretended to be), Blackbird sang out softly,

> "Come out, River, come out of my ear,
> Swirl around the bedroom here.
> Flood the room and float the bed,
> Flow right over the King's head."

Out came River, pour-pour-pouring. All around the room River flowed until the King's bed floated. When the King began to get wet, he sat up and shouted, "For heaven's sake, General Blackbird, take your wife and get out of here!"

So Blackbird found his wife and took her home.

They have lived happily in their tree ever since.

PROPERTY OF
SISKIYOU COUNTY
SCHOOLS LIBRARY

#35389